Welcome to Little Funnies

Little Funnies is a delightful collection of picture books made to put a giggle into storytime.

There are funny stories about a laughing lobster, a daring mouse, a teeny tiny woman, and lots more colourful characters!

Perfect for sharing, these rib-tickling tales will have your little ones coming back for more!

TEE HEE!

HA HA!

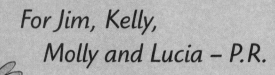

For Jim, Kelly,
Molly and Lucia – P.R.

For Nick – S.H.

First published 1996 by Walker Books Ltd
87 Vauxhall Walk, London SE11 5HJ

The edition published 2007

10 9 8 7 6 5 4 3 2 1

Text © 1996 Phyllis Root
Illustrations © 1996 Sue Heap

This book has been typeset in Highlander Book.

Printed in China

British Library Cataloguing in Publication Data:
a catalogue record for this book is
available from the British Library.

ISBN 978-1-4063-0789-4

www.walkerbooks.co.uk

THE HUNGRY MONSTER

Written by
Phyllis Root

Illustrated by
Sue Heap

Earth MAP

WALKER BOOKS
AND SUBSIDIARIES
LONDON · BOSTON · SYDNEY · AUCKLAND

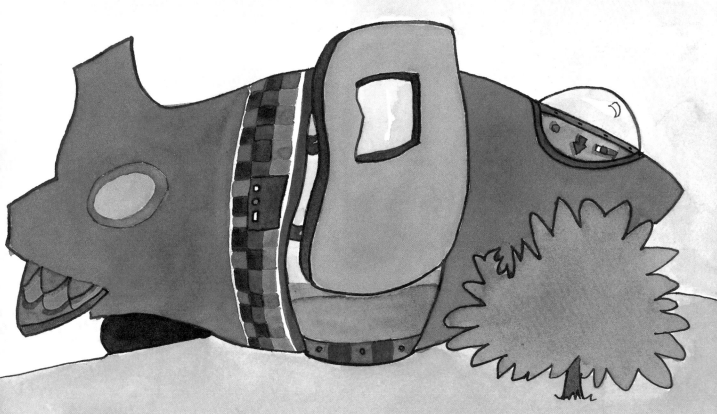

A rocket came to Planet Earth.
Out stepped a monster.

"HUNGRY!" roared the monster.

The monster saw a daisy.
"YUM!" said the monster.

The monster tasted the daisy.

"YUCK!" said the monster.

"REALLY HUNGRY!"
roared the monster.
The monster saw a rock.
"YUM!" said the monster.

The monster tasted
the rock.

"YUCK!" said the monster.

"REALLY, REALLY HUNGRY!"
roared the monster.
The monster saw a tree.
"YUM!" said the monster.

The monster tasted the tree.

"YUCK!" said the monster.

"REALLY,
REALLY,
REALLY
HUNGRY!"
roared the monster.

The monster saw a girl...

"**YUM!**" said the monster.

The monster ate the banana,
skin and all.

"YUCK!" said the girl.

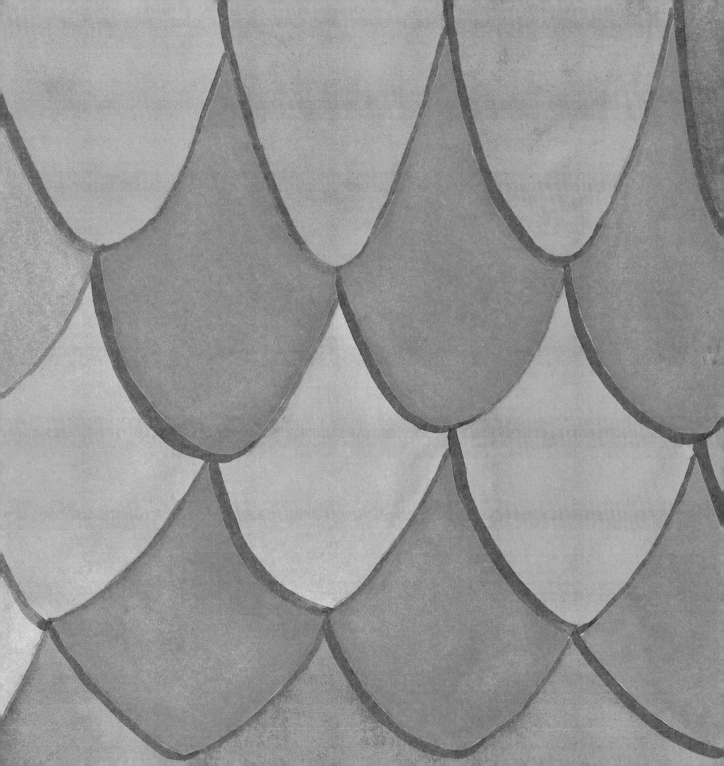